Betsy Hearne

Love Lines

Poetry in Person

Margaret K. McElderry Books
NEW YORK

To my family . . .
MICHAEL EUGENE CLAFFEY
MICHAEL CUCHULAIN CLAFFEY
CYRUS COLUMBKILLE CLAFFEY
JOANNA MEGAN HEARNE
ELIZABETH MARGARET CLAFFEY
. . . poetry in perpetual motion

Margaret K. McElderry Books
Macmillan Publishing Company
866 Third Avenue
New York, NY 10022
Collier Macmillan Canada, Inc.

Composition by Fisher Composition, Inc.
New York, New York
Printed and bound by Fairfield Graphics
Fairfield, Pennsylvania
Designed by Barbara A. Fitzsimmons

First Edition

Printed in the United States of America

10 9 8 7 6 5 4 3 2 1

Library of Congress Cataloging-in-Publication Data
Hearne, Betsy Gould.
Love lines.
Summary: Fifty-nine poems about love—romantic,
friendly, familial—and the loss of love.
1. Love poetry, American. [1. Love—Poetry.
2. American poetry] I. Title.
PS3558.E2554L6   1987   811'.54   87-1737
ISBN 0-689-50437-3

INTRODUCTION

"To make poetry," in the Inuit language, is the same word as "to breathe." Poetry is part of us. If you took away poetry, there would be holes in the human language. Love, too, is crucial to the fabric of living, from childhood to old age. It is woven of many feelings— romantic, erotic, egotistic, nurturant. Love poetry can be benevolent or bitter, sweet or strong or sad. Whatever the texture, there is no better net of words to catch the complexities of loving.

The poems in this collection are about love or the absence of it. The first section is about lovers, friends, and others. The second is about child and family, from which evolves the primary love for yourself that is passed on in turn to your children. The third is about separation, loss, and death. No poem fits neatly into one niche. The themes of the poems, like the emotions of any experience, are a mixture.

Poetry and love both have a music of their own. Love sets the loved ones in a place apart, yet deeply connects them to the rest of the world. Poetry is a pace and space apart, too, but never distant. A few lines a day will keep you company. Like lovers, it is the quality, not the quantity, that counts. Like love, poetry takes time. It takes time to write (these fifty-nine poems were written, with others, over a period of twenty-five years) and time to read. Poems consumed in gulps are boring, even numbing. But if they're sipped, the lines slip into your mind to fit the feelings whenever they come back.

Sometimes, when a song exactly suits what you're feeling, you want to listen to it over and over instead of hearing other songs. It may be simple, but surprisingly apt. Poetry is the same way. Sometimes you want to repeat the same lines instead of moving into other moods and tempos. If only one of these poems touches you in that way, it will last you a long time, exactly like someone you love.

Lovers, Friends, and Others

LOVE LINES

Sometimes love rhymes.
The lines in your face and hands
rhyme with mine, the lines
of our bodies easily entwine,
the lines of our minds fine-tuned
to similar rhythms.
                    In time
you have lined the space of my living like
a string sculpture infinitely extended,
a design that defines our space with
gracious whorls and swirls and spheres of
shining strands soft-spun, silken lariats
that sail across skies, catch clouds on the fly,
a magical rope that unbinds and sets free,
yet doubles as a life line on the sea.
Our feats are not lettered in epics—
love is not metered in regular beats,
but when it's refined,
sometimes love rhymes.

RIVERLOVE

Magic river rounding mountains down,
aqua eyes so speckled in the sun
that I expect wet trout to leap
into my listening mouth. I
wait all day beside the stream
of speech you spill, till suddenly
you're still, in pools of thought or kisses
rounding mountains moments afterwards
with constant flow quite wonderful.
You give me gifts of movement like my own,
floating turning over up and down,
without much need of air but breathing
bubbles, brooknymph rolling in and out of
river rounding mountains down,
river making mountains crowned
with stones smoothed out by touches
of your water mind.

FANTASY FRUIT

Pomegranate,
you look within
as I love within
when he nears,
mouth and hands
slipping over me. Then
I am full of blood,
ripe, round, ready
to open. Taste.

SPRING

You make love like thunder   Roll across the body
                    one more time
                Tongues of lightning flick along my sky
morningsun and midnightmoon both wheel behind my
                    eyes
reflected from your mind   We shake the earth
                Your smile drops softly on my face
seeds buried, rooted
                    I'll bear fruit

                kneedeep in dreams of you
                clover and streams of you
                wading through reams of you
                resting my head

THE GARDEN

Among the grasses
we lay laced
with arms and legs and love
dressed in long hair and soft hair and love.

You may come here,
for we're naked, unafraid.
You may come to rest from warring.
Leave your ghosts at the gate.
Soon I'll get up and give you something to eat.

RESTLESS

The heart drum drums
the night drums drum
the wind hollows footsteps
shadowed by catsteps
passing by my window
passing calls through the pounding walls

Leave your narrow bed
find the night veins
walk the strange streets
with the tight muffled beats
find the pulsing night's heart

ON A MOTORCYCLE OFF LIMITS

Clean lines like a clipper ship,
I could sail you far across the sea
or simply rub my hands along your
legs circling the cycle and nip
the back of your neck (accessibly near my mouth),
a delicacy which (since you know me)
please don't mention was my fantasy.

PLAYERS IN CONCERT

Mingling strings even as we cannot touch,
my guitar slides in tune with yours
attentively in tone and time,
sound-kissing before
chords slip over neck and body
toward a rush of song.

LEPRECHAUN

I never hoped to have you,
and yet your silhouette,
back bent to bury gold in my plants,
flushed a covey of wishes.

AFFAIR

We love suspended in the now and then,
and any time I know I cannot hold
you for a while, I think to the eye
of the hurricane where and when we've lain.
Rides we could take down the coast
are all driven through my head, and
splashing the sand or tickling grass,
relishing treats, beating the alarm clock by a kiss.
Others take for granted their day,
yet in our way we're nearer than they,
never losing track of the fact of discretion
but freer behind our fence than wild things.
I hear a song that makes me long to share
some time and touches, reach just empty air,
hold myself together whole, and say
other claims on your attention are okay
while mine is special in its own way.

AFTER THE AFFAIR

Did you dream and wonder in the dark
that I had disappeared and did you feel
that I would fake and run? Take
a pack of matches, set the letters free.
The words I housed us in, go burn them down.
The memories are typed across your eyes.
You'll stare at them and me and I at you
year after year in the privacy of our pain
and relief at meeting, our unceremonious
coupling of hearts, and dream and wonder
in the dark how short a time it takes to find
someone's center, hold it from then on
with just a flash of curling hair or certain
gait of runners near the lake to be
completely covered with your smile,
shape, fingers, feeling dreams—
and wonder in the dark, the spark, the brief
holding near, while midnight falls apart
and two friends dream and wonder in the dark.

ADVICE

Try making love in a bed or a tub
or leaning against a pillar on top of the Acropolis
some deserted night under a white moon over white
stones the bones of Athens with her living lovers
seething in streets below
Descending afterwards like gods to the sea
with a bottle of wine   Pause near the Forum
and feel your head reel

MARCH WAY

A streetful of wind and of people.
A heartful of childhood and big city.
We mask a skip with dignity,
pull a smile over soulshouts.
Only our eyes dance openly,
our hands tight lightly.
We walk the sun on a leash,
tugging to run after shadows.
We turn aside from somber eyes
to a hillside park.

Four legs dangle down
from a moss-stuck stone wall,
swinging heels, thump, swing.
As far as we can see is world
and sometimes a red poppy.
We sit awhile in dreamtalk,
then jump down
and race to the first flower.
Together we run.

AT WORK

In my office of paper and plants
I lost a mind,
maybe mislaid but
probably blown out the window,
stuck in the sun somewhere, or more
likely lying under your golden body—
unfiled thoughts turn up there.

TWOSOME

Hi, partner,
I called but you weren't home
so here I sat alone with the phone
and a seductive singing record player
all wired like my brain
complex but simple to unplug
once you find the outlet in the wall.

Let's soften things, it's
blazing in here, noisy and
uncaressing. Bring your body in,
fur and freckles, I'll surrender
completely once we turn off time
to find our hidden rhythms,
my ease on you balancing
yours on me—an old scale—
both sides golden
givetaking converged
we have come even.

A DIALOGUE WITH PRIDE

Okay go away
who wants to stay
with a fool?

I have blown my cool.
My friend is gone
to the other room in anger.

We could reconcile
for the world is wide,
the couch narrow.
And if in the imbecility of disagreement you died,
I would wither on my stalk of pride.

What a dry way to die.
It's true we fight
but left alone unloved
we'd fight ourselves—
come see, I've steeped some tea.

DREAMTIME

Watch the wild waters
where the fountain froth falls,
smell the sea searing in the sun,
listen to my harp play,
hear your smoking pine-fire pray,
catch the flying thistledown,
touch the moonlight's gliding gown,
drink the tiger lilies' dew,
know my love,
my love is you.

NOCTURNE

Summer rain and
waiting for you to come to bed
dripping and
turning over and over
thunder and quick lightning
the thrust of you under the sheet
quieting down
my heart slows
the sky slumps and I am slipping
into the partway past of dreams
still slung together with you and
the sound of sleeping storms

THE OLD COUPLE

A violet night
with stars blooming in the grass,
moon floating across spring pools.
We bend together gathering moments
slowly softly as the wind breathes,
wander in sleepful waking,
no walls of flesh or mind,
not even garden gates,
only open and one.

Beside the dawn we hold
a bunch of wilted night.
However, seeds sowed flower.
We will find sometime, some end of day
another violet night.

TWILIGHT GOSSIP

A fogphantom swam inland past the swans.
He circled the swallowtailed air, blew in the rabbit's
                ear,
kissed quiet a thicket of crickets expressing opinions
on women who vie for foglove—lush meadow, sly
shore, sky.
It was the vine, not I, who heard
and repeated it to the pine, who rubbed
and hugged the mooning wind, who stroked
me and mine entwined in bed and told in turn
of fogphantoms swimming inland past the swans,
circling the swallowtailed air, licking the rabbity grass,
kissing quiet a thicket of crickets expressing opinions
on three sighing sisters' damprising desire—
the softening meadow, the swelling shore,
               the spreading sky.
No light is in sight but the white wild rose,
no sound but a long horn that lows of those phantoms
swimming past swans now dark in repose.

First Person, Family, Home

KALEIDOSCOPIC TODDLER

I dismiss the hands that turn my toy world.
I jump from one glass fragment to another
and change whole unrelated orders
with each step.

PLAYING

In my days of flour-sack dresses,
I kept house with a tortoise and mouse
Among the rooms of tree roots.
They passed me secrets over cake and tea,
The mystery of quick and slow,
Of when to pull in my head
And when to go.

ONCE ON A TIME

Walking along little
day after day with
no one to play with
I fell in a hole of
loneliness
it's quite dark and
my knees are still bleeding

OPENING I

"Eye for an eye, tooth for a tooth,"
quoted the sire in defense of his ire,
but his self-centered child
heard "an eye for an I,"
learning early to prize
insight highly.

DOCTOR

Riding roadward
Pa and I paid calls.
He cured sick men
and I kept company.
We sang and played,
pretended rich,
talked snooty what we'd do
with money.

He aged less than I.
We watched car-lights
gobble up black dragon macadam;
watched the southern sun
drink the road grasses' water
till they curled and crackled;
heard silence suck up afternoons
while worried family friends
swatted flies and children,
and he fixed bones and wounds.

Long later I found hearts he lanced,
and learned the crack in the man,
and knew my mother's pain,
waiting at home.

DAD AT DINNER

I look at you
suddenly cracked open
for the space of a collapsed face,
white face lapsed a second,
eyes, mouth, stomach circled
with exhaustion, and wonder
what is our fuel?
Is it food we are looking for?
Love, order?
I had saved something to
tell you, but it fell in the
crack of your face. Something
about myself and my own circles
but, looking at you,
ask who's to blame
for our same world?

MOTHER

Stuck in the cracks
and crevices of her time
broods genius,
and cannot wing or soar.
She has a nesting mind.

GRANDMOTHER, UNDRESSING

Scars of experience stretch
across stomach and thighs, those
active receptacles, crisscrossed
in service of the ego and of
others. We are not perfect,
they proclaim, but we continue.
We have been filled to overflowing and emptied,
poured and quaffed. We've swapped
a smooth surface for the eternity
of infants, interrupted nights, and messy days.
We are marred and marching on.

GRANDFATHER, FAILING

Confusion is a rabbit-running thing,
tearing and wearing, worrying your will,
circling with an iron ring
the freedom leaping way. You're
tensing smaller to a run,
blind-eyed, shrill-shrieking,
frantic-trapped, world-whing
BANG

REFLECTIONS

My brother, my braggart,
you gave our sister a Christmas prism
which whirls and twirls in her room
and dances and catches her fancy
and fetches her eye with hues
and lights and shapes that slide
along its glass surface, like you.

DAUGHTERS

Mothers bend down
like brown grass.

Green, we seeds
sink roots, drip dew,
grow into sundresses,
stiffen in frostsilver coats,
bow brown.

Underground, under grass,
waits the earthen past.

FLEDGLING

In, looking out,
is love-lined.
Walls hold out the wind,
they nest the robin-egg blue,
the thin-shelled dreams holding
promise of flight.

Look out.
Winter window crystals
befeather bare branches
with fork-tongued spring,
with wishes of winging away
over glittering ground.

MARRIAGE

You wrap around my days,
our nights are a gift.
I have opened you, I am wearing you now,
warm as wool. Your words fit exactly around my ears.
It's hard not to hope we can hold off north
memories blowing on the window.

HOPEFUL

Above our bed
rain Philippine bells of shell
translucently.
A raffia, round-woven sun-star
shines strawgold,
lightning-zagged in purpleorangegreen,
Arab basket bearing fruits and grain.

Above me
shine your night eyes.
Body talk, mind talk, tongue talk settle our bed,
and from it spiral paths, rivers, winds.
One of these trips, my friend,
we'll find a child—the common road,
the branching bridge of
roads from end to end.

UNDER THE DOWN COMFORTER

Winter requires several layers,
but we have acquired central heat,
two warm spots insulated so
there is never need to freeze.
Surrounded by cold sometimes, we
are now, however, three,
the third a heater,
heartbeat so new that when we wear thin,
hers will hearten the world as ours
have.
        And I wrap around you now
with all else peeled away, still
fingering the fabric of layers,
uncovered, covering, loving
the feel of invisible wrappings
fallen away.
            Your pasta, chianti,
coffee, cats, stories still stirring
my blood, nursing the baby second-hand;
my own wine of work and worry nursing her first;
hand-in-hand we sleep, stripped of all
but warmth, fantasies, familiarity.
                    Family.

INFANT

Years of you belong to me,
times you will never remember are
mine: nursing with nightlights
of city windows and signs,
holding you up to watch the rain
begin to splash on the pane of glass,
catching expressions cross your face
which will never happen again
for you in your mirror-conscious days.

Later when you grow on
I will not ask
you to stay behind,
for this is my time.
Later I will be gone.

FOUR-YEAR-OLD

You really got into it,
your red raincoat, rainhat
with the red bandanna
to keep out thunder.
You really got into it, your red
sneakers soaking up puddles,
both feet at a time.
Carefully aiming your green water
pistol at every passing tree,
you really got into it, rain
slanting down from your red
sky.
Can I stay out forever, you asked,
fresh from the grass? Yes.
Yes.
You really got into it.
Can I even spend the night? No.
No.
You must come in then.
You will have to come in.

CHILDREN

you are what you are in the eye of the other
yet no one other can reflect each facet of your
                    diamond self
you will shine differently in each setting
and still the gem remains in changing reflections
                    the same

THE LONELY CAT

My kitten cattily independs
along feline tradition,
but, succeeding in seclusion,
saddens.

A sly eye (independent of its golden twin)
opens, discerning my antics. It's
followed by the stretch
of a daily increasingly sexy leg,
as a young lady admiringly draws on
her first nylon stockings,
independently, of course.

The black body straightens,
springs, stiffly stalks a step
and moves with casual dignity
into proximity.

Missing,
Lost, and Beyond

WINTER AWAY

Along the streams of silver sky
I am lonely,
calling for the touch of you
so I may feel thoughts
that you will not speak.
Here on your hand,
I will know you are happy;
here on your thigh,
I will know that you cry.
But the winds will rise,
oh the winds are rising now,
and the little veined petals become chill.

STAYING BEHIND

I did not fold my life
in drawers when you left
but wore it too neatly and worked.

I knitted my days
but couldn't find yarn
to match your particular shade.

I ate my eggs and shaved my legs
and weighed the same on scales
but felt a bit off balance

sitting on the seesaw
by myself.

HOTEL

The night has cracked apart.
I wait in the jagged-edged nerves of dark
for you, alone for you,
hoping to fold in your chestwarm nest
from the olden dark that creeps from
that other side of the room. What
I feel is someone far, the sound of no breathing,
the bed broken in half,
and sleep is an arm reaching.

AN ACQUAINTANCE WITH CHEAP TEARS

The first and last
time you made me cry was
on a whiff of discomfort after dinner.
You said there's no real feeling between us
and damaged the bud.
By now you have a hothouse
high with weeping, fooling, fun.
You can always score by watering one
more but you lost me.
You relate but can't wait.
You're in touch with too much.
Nature has secrets growing underground.
I am made of roots as well as sun.

FIRST LOVE—LATER ON

Rain ringing street lamps
carves lovers leaning lightly in the night,
shapes memories of us
in first flush.

Raindrops fall
and tears,
with a sprinkled distinction,
some salted sadness.
You have come and gone.

Raining writes a million poems.
What need of my falling?

SEX HEX

Watch it babe the bogeyman'll get you
for living before wedding. When
you feel those urgent stirrings
turn your sundrunk eyes into
your wing and don't touch men
you'll fly you'll cry you'll die then.

Mind you don't lick
taste of spring off dripping maple trees
(they watch and catch you walking in the night)
nor lie on your back in wild fields of wind,
of windmaddened grass, to open your thighs
to his thrust, the blunt insistent head of his desire.

Should his hard hands wander softly,
touch him once and toss him
lightly over your shoulder.
Sink the smiles that rise
at whistles in the streets.
Hide from his kindled eyes,
run from his red tongue
the way you do from lightning—
between sheets.

THE CALL

I have touched poems, warm men and wild to dance
begged to. The elder fears said no.
But beating wings have brushed me.
I have felt their wind in my valley
and cannot stay home and cannot go,
but must flit shadowly
along the low unleapt wall
back and forth and back again.

VIOLATION IN RECOLLECTION

Spring seems handsome
but spring brings pain.
His winds strip lilac blooms
and rape the buxom bushes.
Warm air bears sharp remembering.

DEPRESSION

Ladies and gentlemen I
stand with the broken sun in my hand.
Take it away take it away take it away.
It rose in my mind and
set in the mud. It
defies the skies
of even spring.
It is called by the false Freud
father
mother lover son society screwed
but is really traceless and weighs
nothing
a pretender
a weightless ton of lead
ballbearing unhappiness
straining the heart
stringing the shoulders and knotting the neck
killing killing and filling
the desperate empty eyes
with dull rolling tears
    dull rolling tears
fear and death and dull rolling tears.

LOST GENERATION

I have within me
much of my father,
so much of my mother.
But I cannot divorce myself.

GIFTS

In my closet
are six rich coats
my mother bought
to guard me
from the inner cold.

In my bank
are numbered checks
my father signed,
saying please endorse
his love.

EXPLANATION TO THE PALE-FACED
MUTATION OF THE FUTURE

And there was light.
And there was life.
And there was Adam.
And there was Atom.
And there was darkness.

REBIRTH

I spit out my heart
for the rivers of blood and grief
it poured through my body.
I stepped on my heart
to stop the pulse that beat
too fast, too hard against approachers.

That heart reddened my mind,
blinded me in a sunset of tangled veins,
lovelust and tears streaming through the clouds,
a muscle squeezing me beyond all points of pain,
growing me old.
I threw out my heart in the trash.

Yet some morning I might wake earlier
than usual, than the city, and hear in peace
a faint trembling thump newborn
from its broken other.
I'd be terrified and thrilled—
ready, even, to rise again.

SUICIDE

My friend
did you feel so farflung
on the horizons of your mind
that you could not come back
that springtide night
when the silencer covered your tracks
till too late for discovering?
You went out of reach
and meant every step of it.
We waited at school
but you never came
having permanently walked out of class.
Helplessly feeling your dark face
hide the darker heart behind,
who could place blame on your aiming
a bullet at your pain?
Had we known, we'd have kept you
from being alone that time
with that particular intention,
but you needed someone more frequently
than to prevent dying.

MEMORIAL DAY DC-10
(To a Departed Friend)

Silk-shirted woman with Chinese skin
you have passed into oblivion, torn in
a terrible tenuous flight unlike
the glides you made down Michigan
Avenue, eyefully, eloquently, exquisitely
patterning your people and places in
unique blend. There has been, since then,
no one designed like you.

                            Quickly you went,
but backward, cloth to moth, one second
dressing for the plane, the next, naked
on fire. We are left with the fabric
unfinished.

                I will never feel silk
without you slipping through the fingers
of my mind. Silk is suddenly the quality
of come and gone.

SONG

Mourning doves know parting.
They fly away
and cry in the cool dusk
remembering
the soft closeness of feathers.

AFTER THE FUNERAL

You look lonely in black,
with myriad colors arching past.
You sit shadowed,
the ghosts in your face conversing.
Red bubbles by,
blue splashes,
green rustles,
yelloworange smokes.
Yet there you sit darkened,
with blinds drawn over your lighted eyes.

HOMESICK

My sleep is barren on the bed,
my eyes have forgotten the stars,
my feet, the lift of the mountains.
The monument clouds build and tumble,
shape, reshape, and fade away.

The sidewalk grass grows crackling
broken glass in pointed patches.
Remember the sticky itching kind
we rolled on down the hills,
the grass that bent sweetscented?

PERENNIAL

Slight white flowers of the night sky
blink against galactic winds,
expending their scent beyond our ken.
We point to their petals past the rim
of vision, extending wishes to them
like cosmic rain reversed to nourish
godly garden beds. The stars
are still our covenant with spring.

        a n
      l   d
     n am i
    o   r   i   n
   o y   d g
  m p   s s